The Pregnant Amish Quilt Maker

Hannah Schrock

Table of Contents

Clearfield County, Pennsylvania, Early March...

Eve looked up from the quilting frame as the bell over the door to the small quilt shop tinkled, letting her know a new customer had just entered the store. She watched as two Englisch women slowly wandered around the shop, gently fingering the quilts displayed on wooden hangars.

"Oh, I just love the colors in this one," the younger of the two women remarked. "I could never sew like this."

"This is one of the best reasons to visit here," the other woman remarked. She looked up, spying Eve sitting in the opposing corner and smiled at her.

"Good morning. Are these your quilts?"

Eve stuck her needle in the fabric to she wouldn't lose her place and stood up, smoothing the black apron down as she walked around the wooden frame, "Some of them. Many women in the Amish communities around here display and sell their quilts in this shop."

"Well, I have to tell you I'm so jealous of your talent. Do you happen to know who made the purple and blue wedding ring quilt there?" The younger woman pointed back to the quilt that had first captured her attention.

Eve smiled at her, "That is one of mine. It is a wedding ring pattern."

"Yes, and the colors are so vibrant." The woman shared a smile with her, "My sister is getting married at the end of the month and I wanted to get her and my future brother-in-law something extra special. I think that quilt would make a wonderful wedding gift."

Eve inclined her head, "I will fit a king sized bed."

"Perfect! I'll take it."

"Wunderbaar!" Eve wrote up the ticket and was pleased to see that the women had indeed come prepared with cash. So many of the Englisch came to the small shops expecting to use their credit cards or write checks. While some of the shops that were owned by the Englisch accepted credit cards, the Amish-owned stores did not.

She carefully removed the quilt from the hangar and lovingly folded it, before placing it inside the brown paper sack. "Denke," she told the women as they happily received their purchase and left the shop.

Eve rubbed her temples, hoping the Jeremiah was already on his way to pick her up. She had married Jeremiah King the previous November, and even now she was amazed at how she'd changed.

Eve had met Jeremiah when he had come to her parents' quilt shop, where she worked, to repair a leaky roof. Her daed had recently injured his knee and when Jeremiah had stopped by to offer his assistance, he'd gladly accepted the help.

Eve had been twenty-two at the time, and Jeremiah had been twenty-four, just recently celebrating his birthday a few weeks earlier. He was a cabinetmaker and carpenter in his daed's shop and when he and Eve had first met, it had been a case of love at first sight.

The ever independent and headstrong young quilt maker had tried to ignore her attraction to him, but Jeremiah had kept at it, and six months after their first meeting, they had become engaged. Jeremiah had won not only her heart over, but her head as well.

Eve had gladly learned to relinquish control to him, something she knew had made her parents very happy. For far too many years, Eve had insisted on doing things herself, to the point of defect. The other young menner of their Ordnung had found it hard to deal with Eve because she always had an opinion and didn't mind sharing it. An odd trait for most Amish.

Jeremiah, rather than being offended and turned off from pursuing a relationship with her, had seen her independence as a challenge. One he'd gladly met and conquered. She smiled as she thought back to how diligent he'd been in his pursuit of her affections.

Jeremiah was very handsome and she thanked Gott daily for blessing her with such a gut mann. She walked around the small shop, straightening up here and there and then quickly sweeping the wooden floorboards. Before getting married, she would have closed the shop when she wanted and driven herself home, or walked the three miles without complaint.

But Jeremiah was very careful with his fraa and insisted on driving her to and from work. He also had insisted on her keeping standard hours at the quilt shop. Eve had listened to his request and his reasoning and gladly complied. Another change from her normal behavior patterns prior to meeting the love of her life.

Jeremiah had become her world, secondly only to Gott and on days like today, she had trouble remembering what life had been like before meeting him. She was just putting the broom away when the bell over the door announced another visitor.

She stepped out, prepared to announce that the shop was closed, to see Jeremiah standing inside the shop rubbing his hands together briskly. She smiled warmly at him and loved the feeling of her heart speeding up. She was so in love with her husband and she grinned as she remembered they were going to have an indoor picnic today to celebrate the day they had first met.

It had been Jeremiah's idea and one she'd wholeheartedly agreed with. It was much too cold to have a picnic outdoors just yet, but that wouldn't stop them from pretending and enjoying being with one another. Jeremiah had built them a lovely home and she was looking forward to putting in a garden, come springtime, and helping her husband pick out the farm animals they would add at that time.

"Ready to go?" Jeremiah asked, leaning forward and kissing her cheek. Public displays of affection were frowned upon in their community, but Jeremiah never ceased to greet her in the same way. It had drawn more than one smirk and raised brow from the elders in their Ordnung, but Eve found she didn't really mind. She loved knowing that Jeremiah cared for her and had missed her while they were apart.

"Jah. It was a gut day, I sold another quilt."

"That's great news. One of your own?"

"Jah. An Englischer bought it as a wedding present for her sister. Are we still having our picnic?" she asked, thinking ahead to the things she still needed to do to complete their evening meal.

"We are and I have another surprise for you," he told her as she locked the quilt shop door. He led her to his buggy and handed her up, pulling the thick lap blanket from behind the seat and tucking it around her legs.

Eve watched him jog around the horse, climbing into the buggy a moment later. "What kind of surprise?"

Jeremiah winked at her, "I stopped by the diner and had Mary Anne put together a picnic dinner for us. You, my lovely bride, do not have to cook tonight."

Eve leaned over and kissed him on the cheek, "Denke. That is a very nice surprise."

Jeremiah reached for her hand, and started them on their journey home. Eve sat back and enjoyed just being with her husband. One day they would have a familye to take care of, and she was following a piece of advice given to her by her mamm on her wedding day. Enjoy the time you have with your husband alone, for once the children start arriving, finding time alone with one another will take much work.

Eve was doing her best to heed that advice. And she'd never been happier.

One week after the accident…

Eve woke up, lying in her bed as the sunlight filtered beneath the curtains and wondered what was the use in even crawling from her bed. It had been eight days since the love of her life had died, and with each passing day, she wished she'd died with him.

She didn't even feel guilty for having such thoughts. Each day, a steady stream of family and friends came to her door and tried to get her to talk to them. And each day, she ignored them and refused to see anyone. She slid her legs over the side of the bed, feeling nauseous and slightly dizzy, but that had become the normal for her. Even before Jeremiah had died.

She took several deep breaths and then gingerly stood up, holding onto the mattress until the room around her quit spinning. She pulled her robe on and slowly made her way towards the kitchen. Dirty dishes sat on the butcher block next to the sink, but instead of feeling guilty for not having cleaned up after herself, she turned away from them and wandered over to the window.

The sun was shining, and she could see that someone had been faithfully tending to her garden. She turned away and slowly made her way over to the kitchen table and sat down. Her Bible was sitting just out of reach and she shook her head. What's the use? Gott doesn't care about me! He gave me Jeremiah and then he took him away? What kind of Gott does that? Not one that truly cares for me.

She laid her head on her arms and cried. She cried for the loss of Jeremiah. She cried for the loss of her best friend and the man she'd thought to spend her life growing old with. She cried because for the loss of her faith in Gott.

A knock on the back door startled her and she lifted her head, glancing through the crack in the curtain to see her parents standing there, looking extremely worried.

"Eve! We know you can hear us. Dochder, please open the door and speak to us."

She could hear the worry in her daed's voice and felt bad for worrying them so. She walked to the door and opened it a crack. She looked horrible and her mamm gasped at the sight of her looking so wan.

"Eve! You've not been eating."

"I have," she told her with a weak smile. "I just…I just need a few more days."

"You need to rejoin the living. Jeremiah wouldn't want you acting like this."

Eve felt tears fill her eyes, acknowledging that her daed was right. Jeremiah would have been disappointed in her if he saw her like this. When they'd first met, she'd been so independent, but looking at her now, she was weak and had completely lost her will to move forward.

"Daed I appreciate your concern, I truly do."

"Eve, you need to come back to the quilt shop. Even if just for a few hours," her daed suggested.

"Not today. Maybe later in the week…"

Her parents looked at her and after a lengthy pause, her daed nodded his head and stepped back. "Three more days."

Eve nodded her head, "Three days. I will come to the quilt shop…"

Her daed shook his head decisively, "Nee. You will come to the haus for dinner. That will be enough. The quilt shop will come in time."

Eve felt tears fill her eyes again and she nodded, "Denke." Her mamm stepped forward and wrapped her in a hug and Eve allowed the contact. But only for a few seconds. Her nausea had returned and she suddenly had a strong desire to be by herself. She stiffened, by no fault of her own as her stomach revolted and then pushed away, stepping back inside the haus hurriedly. "I'll see you in three days."

She hastily closed the door and made her way over to the kitchen sink, breathing heavily as she fought the nausea that had come back full force. She lost the battle a few seconds later, emptying her stomach in great heaves that had tears streaming from her eyes.

When she was finished, she rinsed her mouth out and then methodically cleaned out the sink before heading back to her bed. She laid down, closing her mind off to everything as she allowed her sorrow and depression to overwhelm her. She didn't allow her sickness to take up even a second more of her thoughts, nor did she think about the fact that three days from now she was expected to put on a brave face and join her parents for dinner. She didn't think about anything.

*****

Two days later, Eve ran for the sink once again, emptying her stomach of the dry toast and apple she'd eaten fifteen minutes earlier. This was the third morning in a row where she'd awakened nauseated and then ended up throwing up right after eating breakfast.

She lifted her head and held onto the edge of the sink as the room spun crazily around her. She breathed deeply a few times and then tried to stand up straight, relieved when both her stomach and her equilibrium seemed to have returned to normal.

She rinsed the sink out and then took her lukewarm tea out to the front porch. Tomorrow she was supposed to leave the haus and she wasn't sure she'd be able to do it. She didn't want to see the rest of the world. Not without…

She stopped her thoughts and sat down in the rocking chair. She pushed off, watching nothing. She sipped her tea, and watched the birds frolicking in the apple tree to her right. She set her teacup down and began to worry the apron she'd donned out of habit while getting dressed this morning.

When she realized what she was doing, she clenched her fingers tight and then began to smooth the wrinkles out of the black fabric. When she reached her stomach and smoothed her hand over the apron's pleats, she slowed her hand as her heart stopped beating for a moment.

She moved her hand over her stomach once again and suddenly the truth that she had been ignoring for the last six weeks became clear. She was pregnant!

There was no mistaking the slight protrusion. She looked down at her body in disbelief. She'd been ignoring the signs, not wanting to acknowledge that she was indeed with child, but those days were now over. She wasn't showing enough that others would be able to tell, but she knew deep inside her heart that she was… carrying Jeremiah's boppli.

She burst into great heaving sobs. "Gott! How could you do this to me?"

She looked at the heavens and raised her voice, "This is not fair! Not only did you take my husband, by now my child will grow up without a father!"

She cried until there were no more tears to shed; until her head ached and her heart felt like it had bled itself dry. What am I supposed to do now? Gott! Answer me that!

Two weeks later…

Eve looked up from the quilt frame where she was piecing together her newest creation. It had been a long two weeks, but she was starting to get back into her old routine once again. Minus the dead husband who no longer took her to the shop and then retrieved her at the end of the day.

She now walked to the shop, or caught a ride in her daed's buggy. The buggy Jeremiah had been driving the night he died had been destroyed when the large truck struck them. The horse had survived unharmed, but had been residing in her daed's stable since that time.

Eve had received several offers from other Ordnung members of a replacement buggy, but right now she'd not taken any of them up on those kind gestures. She would need to soon, but until then, she was happy to walk.

"Can I help you?" she asked the older Englisch couple who were quietly whispering to

one another as they looked at the quilt displayed around the small shop.

"These are marvelous!" the woman told her with a smile.

"Denke. Were you looking for something in a particular color?" Eve asked, the salesperson in her coming forth.

"Well, my grandmother had this lovely quilt on her bed while I was growing up. I was hoping to find something similar to it…"

"Could you describe what it looked like?" Eve suggested with a smile.

"Yes. There were large circles of fabric, interwoven together…"

"It sounds like a classic wedding ring pattern." Eve walked to the other side of the shop and picked up a dark green and golden yellow quilt, "Did it look something like this?"

The woman clapped her hands, "That's it! Oh, Jim, we found it!"

Eve smiled at the woman's enthusiasm, "Was there a particular color scheme you were looking for? We have several quilts in various sizes and colors in this pattern."

"One that would fit a king bed and in a navy blue would be perfect."

Eve smiled and then opened a chest on the floor and withdrew a king sized quilt in the wedding ring pattern, with dark navy and cornflower blue circles. "How about this one?"

"Jim that would be perfect, don't you think?"

"Whatever you want dear. We'll take it," the man told her, pulling his wallet from his pants pocket. "What's the total?"

Eve carried the quilt over to the counter and wrapped it in brown paper and then placed it inside a brown paper sack. She gave the man the total and then nodded at them as they left the shop, the woman almost in tears she was so happy with her purchase.

Eve returned to her quilting frame, thinking how something never changed. The Englisch came to their small part of the world to see how the Amish lived and to carry home with them souvenirs. Some purchased furniture. Some ate at the small diner and took home a recipe book, handwritten, and containing recipes that would never taste quite like the meal or dessert they'd eaten at an Amish diner.

And others purchased small wooden toys, or quilts, everything handmade and rare in the world they lived in where everything was made in another country. The Amish didn't use electricity, so everything was handmade in the purest sense of the term. Hard work and long hours went into their goods, and the Englisch didn't mind paying a premium price for the ability to own some of them.

The bell over the door rang out again and she looked up to see her mamm stepping inside the shop. She carried a handful of quilts over her arm, some of them quilts that Eve had almost finished prior to Jeremiah's death and that her mother had finished.

"Gutentag mamm."

"Gutentag, Eve." Her mamm gave her a discerning look and then nodded, "You look much better today. Are you feeling more your old self?"

"Jah. I am doing better." Eve had always been a resilient person, never allowing illness or circumstances to keep her down for long. Her reaction to Jeremiah's death had been unusual for her, and her mamm had been justifiably concerned. "Denke for finishing the quilts."

"No worries, dochder." She looked at the new quilt and smiled, "That is a new pattern."

"A very hard pattern," Eve told her with a hint of her old spirit. She'd never been known for taking the easy road and had decided to do this particular pattern because of its difficulty level.

"It will be beautiful when finished."

Eve inclined her head in acknowledgement of the comment. Her mamm busied herself hanging up the new quilts and then she left to complete some purchases at the stores in town. "I'll be waiting with the buggy by the gazebo in the town square when you're ready to go home."

Eve nodded and watched her mamm leave. Guilt assailed her as she found herself questioning Gott once more. Why couldn't you let Jeremiah live so that we could both raise this boopli I carry? I wanted a familye. Now I am a widow and going to be a single mother.

She felt tears sting her eyes and she quickly wiped them away. She had been trying to rebuild her faith for the last several days. She'd been scouring the Scriptures, trying to find something to hold onto that would help her understand Gott's purpose for her life. Her single life.

She'd read the book of Job, but when she'd come to the part where Gott had restored all that he'd lost, and then some, she'd closed the Bible in defiance. She didn't even want to consider marrying another mann. She'd loved Jeremiah with her whole heart and he would never be replaced.

Just the thought of ever sharing with another what she'd shared with her beloved husband made Eve shake in denial. Jeremiah had been her entire world.

She placed a hand over her stomach and took a deep breath. This boppli was coming, whether she acknowledged it or not. It was still too early for anyone else to tell, but she knew. And she had only a short amount of time left before everyone else who met her would know as well.

Two weeks later…

"Eve, some of the older singles are meeting at Bruder's pond this evening. Why don't you think about joining them?" Fraa Schrock told her dochder as they sat inside the quilt shop on a sunny afternoon.

"Nee. I've no time for such activities…"

"Eve, you need to meet people."

Eve ignored her mamm, knowing full well her mother meant she should be meeting potential husbands. In the Amish world her mamm lived in, a woman wasn't complete if she didn't have a husband and a handful of kinner running around. But Eve couldn't imagine a time in the future, near or otherwise, where she would even consider getting married again.

"Eve?"

"I'm not ready. I don't know if I'll ever be ready." Eve didn't mean to sound upset, but her mamm had been on this subject for several days now. Her mamm was of the opinion that Eve needed to move on. Eve didn't see things that way.

Jeremiah was the only man for her, and just thinking about betraying their love by even entertaining the idea of getting married again felt wrong.

"I see plenty of people here at the shop."

"Those are not the type of people I was talking about," her mamm informed her.

Eve smiled, "I know, but truly, I'm doing okay." In fact, the morning sickness is almost gone now.

Eve still hadn't told anyone that she was expecting a boppli. Jeremiah's boppli to be exact. She was just starting to feel like her old self again, and once word got out that she was expecting, she'd be the object of everyone's well-meaning advice once more. That was not something she was prepared to deal with right now.

"Jeremiah would not want you to be alone…"

"Jeremiah has only been dead for a little over a month, mamm. I think he would be fine with me taking some time to mourn his passing."

Her mamm lowered her eyes and then nodded, "Jah. You are right. You'll know when it is time to meet someone new."

*****

Three weeks later…

Another loud clap of thunder caused Eve to jump in the chair and gaze out the large windows of the quilt shop. It was later afternoon, and had been raining steadily for the past two hours. The sky was dark gray, and even though she knew the sun shone somewhere above the clouds, right now it looked dreary and ominous outside.

"There won't be any more tourists coming in today," she murmured to herself as she stood up from the quilting frame and stretched her arms above her head. Her dressed pulled tight across her ever growing abdomen and she dropped her arms.

She'd need to make herself a few bigger dresses soon, but first she'd finish the quilt she was working on. At home. She'd finally gotten tired of walking everywhere and had accepted a neighbors offer of an older buggy. She'd have to hurry down to the small stable where the Amish boarded their horses and stowed their buggies during the workday, but she wasn't afraid of a little moisture. It was better than walking all the way home through the rain and the mud!

She picked up her stuff and stowed it behind the counter and then headed towards the front door. She straightened up the quilts as she went, preparing to close the blinds and the shop for the day. The Englisch were fair weather shoppers and since it had begun raining earlier in the day, she'd seen fewer and fewer of them walking along the streets of the small town. Closing early would not result in any lost business and she knew her parents would agree with her decision to shut down a few hours early.

She pulled the first two blinds closed, but as she reached for the last one, suddenly the front door burst open and man came barreling inside the shop. Eve turned in surprise, gasping at his appearance.

He was soaked through. And dripping water all over the floor boards! When the wind came howling in after him, forcing the rain sideways and creating a bigger puddle on the floor, she expected him to hastily shut the door, but he just stood there for a moment as if frozen.

Determined to rouse him from his stupor, she raised her voice above the storm, "Shut the door!"

Whether it was the volume of her voice, or the words, he shook himself slightly and then turned and wrestled the door closed. Shutting out the sound of the wind and blocking further rain from coming inside. Closing himself inside with her; the storm raging outside.

Gabriel leaned against the door for a moment and then turned to thank the owner of the shop forgiving him refuge. He grimaced at the large puddle of water that was beginning to form around his feet, "I'm making a mess. I'm sorry…"

His voice trailed off as he lifted his head and got his first good glimpse of his benefactor. She's beautiful. He finally got his brain and his mouth to work, "I'm Gabriel Esh."

The young woman nodded and introduced herself, "Eve King. And you are making a terrible mess on the floor."

"Have you some towels? I can wipe it up…"

"Looking at how wet your clothing is, you would only create another puddle," she told him with a small smile. "I've seen you around the town."

Gabriel nodded, "I've seen you as well." In truth, they had run into each other over the years several times, but had never really spoken to one another. They simply happened to be at the same events.

"I'll get you a towel," she told him and headed for the back room. She emerged a few moments later with a towel. "This will help a little bit."

Gabriel took the towel from her and scrubbed it over his head and face before tossing it to the floor and using his booted feet to wipe up the puddle there. He then stood on the towel, hoping it would soak up the water that continued to drip off his person.

Eve watched him for a moment and then walked over and closed the last blind. "I was just getting ready to close down."

Gabriel looked at her, and then shook his head. She raised a brow at him and he explained, "You can't close the shop yet."

Eve bristled before his eyes, clearly not liking being told what to do. "I don't think you get to have an opinion about when I close the shop."

Gabriel smiled at her, liking the fire in her eyes, but not wanting it directed at her. "No, I meant you can't go out in the storm just yet."

"Why not?" she asked, peeking out the window. A loud clap of thunder that shook the glass was her answer. She jumped back, her heart rate increasing along with the fierceness of the storm.

"The storm is getting worse. It's not safe to be moving around outside."

*****

Eve hated that he was right. She hated the fact that he thought it was his right to tell her what to do even more. But he is only trying to protect you. And you know he's right. No one drives a buggy in this kind of weather. It's asking for lightning to strike or the wheels to get stuck in the mud. Or worse yet, for the horse to get spooked and turn the buggy over.

"It sounds much worse," she grudgingly agreed.

"Jah. We should just wait it out. These types of storms never last long."

Eve nodded, not necessarily agreeing with him. It had been raining for over two hours and seemed to be increasing in intensity, not lessening. Her upbringing kicked in and she turned towards the back of the shop, "Would you like to sit down?"

Gabriel nodded his head, shucking his wet overcoat and pleased to find that he was no longer dripping water. "Denke."

He followed her to the back of the shop and she pulled out another folding chair for him to use. She seated herself and then watched as he placed the damp towel on the chair before sitting down. She smiled, "The chair will dry."

Gabriel looked up and smiled back, "So will I."

She nodded, "So, Gabriel…what do you do?" She was trying to be polite and use the manners her mamm had taught her. After all, she was stuck here with this mann until the storm abated. And truth be told, she'd missed having someone to talk to.

"I build things."

"Build things? Like furniture?" she asked.

Gabriel shook his head, "No, like buildings. Several of the other young men and I build things for the Englisch."

Eve looked at him and then asked, "Do you enjoy working for them? The Englisch?"

Gabriel nodded, "Jah. They pay well and are always wanting to build something bigger and better. It's good steady work."

"That's gut." She grew quiet and then jumped when he started speaking.
"I knew your husband. I've very sorry for your loss."

Eve watched him for a moment and then dropped her eyes. "Denke. I miss him."
"I can only imagine. He was a gut mann." He grew quiet and then asked, "You didn't attend his funeral service?"

Eve shook her head, "I…I could not. I know some people see that as a weakness, but I can't just forget him and move on."
"People are expecting you to do this?" he asked incredulously.

Eve nodded, "My mamm is already hinting that I need to remarry."

Gabriel shook his head, "You should do what your heart tells you to do. Gott doesn't expect any more than that."

Eve looked at him and nodded slowly. She didn't tell him that she wasn't sure Gott even cared. That was almost too personal to share with someone who had been a stranger to her until half an hour earlier.

"So, are any of these your quilts?" he asked, helping her by changing the subject.

Eve took the opening he gave her and nodded, "Yes, right now most of them are mine." She watched as he got up and walked around the small shop, looking at the various quilts with interest.

"These are so elaborate. How do you know which pieces go where?"

Eve smiled, "I use a pattern for the more intricate designs, but a few of the more common ones I could probably make in my sleep."

"Do you enjoy quilting?"

Eve nodded her head, "I like being able to take pieces of fabric and put them together to make something that people enjoy and can use."

Gabriel shared a smile with her, "Well, it seems we have something in common. We both like to build things. You build with cloth and thread, while I build with concrete and wood. Either way, it is very satisfying to see the final product."

Eve nodded at him, liking how well they understood one another. The quiet drew her eyes to the front door and she smiled, "The rain is stopping."

Gabriel turned as well and smiled, "So it is. Eve, it was a pleasure to meet you. Denke for allowing me to drip water all over your floor."

"You are most welcome. You also kept me from going home in the storm."

"You would have come to your senses, but I'm glad I got a chance to meet you. Drive home carefully."

"I will," she assured him.

Gabriel gave her one last look and then waved before stepping through the door and disappearing down the sidewalk. She closed the door and locked it, walking slowly to the back door, her mind still fixed on the handsome young man she'd just spent the last forty minutes talking with.

Forty minutes that she'd actually enjoyed. Gabriel was charming and very easy on the eyes. And he understood what drove her to quilt. That in itself was a rarity and one she found very attractive.

Maybe I'll run into him again sometime. He was nice to talk to.

One week later…

Gabriel stepped into the shop and waved at Eve as she finished collecting money from the Englisch couple standing at the counter.

"Denke. I hope you enjoy the quilt," Eve told them in her soft-spoken voice.

"Oh, we will. We will."

The couple left and Gabriel approached the counter, "Hi."

"Hi," she told him back. "You're not wet today."

Gabriel grinned, "Not a storm cloud in sight. I came to see if you wanted to get some lunch with me."

Eve was shocked and just looked at him for a minute. "Lunch?"

"Yes. Do you get a lunch break?"
"Today I get off at lunch. My mamm will be coming in at 12:30 to work until closing."
"Gut. Join me for lunch?"
"Uhm…I guess…?"

"Don't guess. How about I stop by the diner and pick up some sandwiches and we can eat them in the park? It is a beautiful day outside, the sun is shining, and I hear birds on my way here."

Eve laughed, "That sounds nice."

"Gut. Turkey or ham?"
"Turkey," she told him with a smile. "Shall I meet you at the park?"
"I'll wait for you on the bench at the corner," he told her.

She nodded her head and grinned as he left the shop, holding the door open for the two elderly ladies who were headed inside to look at the quilts. She answered their questions and rang up their purchases, but her head was firmly fixed on the lunch she was going to share with Gabriel.

Her mamm arrived and Eve quickly gathered up her things. She could fee her mamm's eyes following her movements, but she didn't stop to explain or give her a chance to ask a bunch of questions.

She was just having lunch with a new friend. That's all Gabriel was. A friend. She didn't want to fall in love, and wasn't even sure if her heart was capable of doing so this soon. They were just friends, and everyone needed those.

She waved goodbye to her mamm and headed down the sidewalk. Gabriel was already waiting for her and she waved to him.

"Ready to eat?"

Eve nodded, "Very." Since the morning sickness had disappeared, she found herself eating more than normal. Given the speed with which her stomach was expanding, she wasn't surprised.

Gabriel offered his elbow as they stepped to the curb and she took it, trying to ignore how similar the action was to how Jeremiah had looked out for her. She tried not to compare the two menner, but deep inside her heart, she found herself liking having a mann offering her his protection.

They walked to the park and Gabriel led her over to a sunny spot where they could watch the geese floating on the pond in the distance. "Will this do?"

"It's perfect," she told him, gingerly lowering herself to a sitting position on the grass. Once she was seated modestly, she looked up to see Jeremiah watching her with a strange look upon his face.

She smiled at him, "Is there something wrong?"

Jeremiah looked somewhat nervous and then cleared his throat, "Forgive me, but...I don't know how to ask this without seeming like I'm prying."

Eve realized where he was going and nodded, "Jah. I'm pregnant."

"Jeremiah didn't know?" he asked softly, sitting down across from her.

Eve shook her head sadly, "Nee. He would have been so happy…"

"I'm sorry, but I hadn't noticed before…do many people know?"

"Family and a few close friends…everyone will know soon enough. I'm starting to get too big to hide."

"You don't need to hide. And I can see what you are thinking, you are still very beautiful."

Eve blushed, unused to such compliments coming from anyone other than her late husband. She didn't have a chance to respond, as he opened up the sack he'd carried and handed her a wax paper wrapped sandwich and a bag of chips. He also handed her a cold bottle of water and then pulled the exact same thing from a sack for himself.

He didn't ask her a bunch of questions, he simply started eating. She did the same, and was amazed at how relaxed she was in his presence. She truly enjoyed spending time with Gabriel, but that didn't mean she had to fall in love with him. He was her friend. Nothing more.

Three weeks later…

Eve stood looking at the tree limb that lay on the roof and scowled. A fierce wind storm had swept through their little town the night before, and a large branch had broken free of the tree and was now waiting for someone to remove it from the roof.

She'd heard it hit during the small hours of the morning, but with the wind blowing so fiercely, she'd waited until this morning to see what damage had been done. From what she could tell, only a few of the roofing shingles had been torn loose, but that was a few too many.

There was a ladder in the stable, but in her condition, and protruding stomach, she didn't dare risk climbing it to repair the roof or remove the tree limb.

She closed her eyes, tears stinging them as she realized she was helpless to do what needed to be done. If Jeremiah were here, he'd take care of these things and I wouldn't even have to give them a second thought.

This wasn't the first time she'd had such thoughts. Being independent, Eve didn't mind getting her hands dirty, but she was eighteen weeks pregnant and had another life to think of now. Climbing a ladder and walking around on the two-story roof of the house Jeremiah had built involved too much risk to herself and her unborn child.

The sound of a buggy in the drive had her walking around the house to investigate. Gabriel was just climbing from the buggy and he waved and gave her a friendly smile.

She smiled back, "What are you doing here? Don't you have to work today?"

"Jah, but not until later. I thought I would come see if you suffered any damage from the storm last night.

Eve felt a surge of relief, "Actually, a limb broke off the tree and is on the roof…"

Gabriel smiled at her, "Do you have a ladder?"

"In the stable," she gestured over her shoulder.

"Great. Why don't you go back inside and I'll see what I can do about that roof?"

Eve wanted to protest being told to go inside, but her feet were achy and she hadn't had any breakfast yet. Something her stomach was protesting very strongly about. She nodded, "Have you eaten yet?"

"A bit, but I wouldn't turn down more food," he told her with a wink.

Eve grinned back at him, "I will fix breakfast for both of us then." She headed inside and quickly scrambled some of the eggs she'd collected the day before, chickens being the only livestock she and Jeremiah had invested in prior to his death. They'd intended to add a milk cow and some other animals, but life had gone a different direction.

She pulled her thoughts back to the present and placed some bacon in the pan as well.

She heard Gabriel lean the ladder against the haus and then his footsteps on the roof above. Fifteen minutes later, he knocked on the back door and stepped inside, "All fixed."

"Denke. Come eat," she placed two plates on the kitchen table.

He sniffed appreciatively, "It smells gut."

"Don't thank me until you taste it."

Gabriel smiled, "It will be the best I've had in a while because I did not have to cook it." He seated himself, removed his hat and then reached for her hand. She placed hers in his and then bowed her head as he prayed. "Gott, bless this food and the hands that have prepared it. We thank You for protecting Eve's haus from the storm last night and ask that You would help us better to do You will this day. Amen."

They ate in relative silence and then Gabriel helped her carry the dishes to the sink, "I must go now. We are building a six story building and today we start on the top floor."

Six stories? Eve nodded, not asking him how he managed to get any work done so high up off the ground. "Have a gut day. And thank you again for stopping by to check on me. That was very nice."

"I'm a nice guy," he told her with a wink. "I'll see you soon." He replaced his hat on his head and left through the back door. Moments later she heard his buggy pull out of the driveway and she felt strangely deflated that he was gone.

He's a friend. Just a friend. Her self-lecture was interrupted by the feeling of her boppli moving insider her. She placed her hands on her stomach in wonder and then started laughing. Deep belly laughs that stole her breath and made her feel gut inside. This was going to be a gut day after all.

End of August…

The pattern of Gabriel coming by to help out around the haus had become a normal routine and part of Eve's day. Very seldom did a day go by where Gabriel didn't stop by, either in the morning before he headed into the construction site, or just before the sun set, when he was tired and dirty from a hard day's work.

Eve had come to expect his visits, and had even started waiting to eat dinner with him on those days when he didn't come by in the morning.

He fixed things that were broken, helped her put up a fence to keep the deer from devouring what was left of her garden, and he even strung up a new clothesline for her when the old one broke.

She'd finally managed to get over her angst about having to rely on someone else, other than Jeremiah, to do these things for her, and was feeling grateful to Gabriel for his help. And his advice. Today was one of those days when she needed his advice.

Tomorrow was the first Sunday meeting she would be attending where her pregnancy would not be hidden. She was more than halfway through her nine months, and her stomach was more prominent than ever.

Her mamm and her ant had visited earlier in the day, insisting that she couldn't possibly think to raise this child on her own. They had offered their congratulations, but that hadn't been the reason for their visit. They wanted her to get married again. Immediately. They'd even gone so far as to compile a list of eligible widows who wouldn't mind raising another mann's child as his own.

Eve had barely held onto her temper as the two well-meaning women tried to sell her on the idea of getting married again. She'd waited them out, keeping silent until they'd run out of words and come to the realization that she was not having any part in their planning.

She'd been gracious and kind, but had pleaded a headache and the need for a nap, sending them on their way with a promise to give their words some consideration when she was feeling a bit better. She had no intention of thinking about their words. Now or in the future.

But they would not be the only ones wanting to give her advice. After the Sunday meeting, every woman in their Ordnung would feel inclined to do the same thing. Eve wasn't sure she could deal with that. She was toying with the idea of just not going to Sunday meeting, but that would result in the elder bishop paying her a personal visit and having to make a lengthy explanation to her parents. Neither of those options was any more appealing than dealing with a bunch of unasked for advice.

"What has you so pensive tonight?" Gabriel asked as they

finished dinner and sat on the front porch.

Eve sighed, "My mamm and ant came by this morning. They want me to marry again."

Gabriel was very silent and she looked at him, swallowing nervously when she saw him watching her with so much emotion in his eyes and on his face.

"Eve, surely you know how I feel about you by now?" he asked softly, taking her hand between his own.

She looked down at their joined hands and nodded, "Jah. I know."

"I love you."

Eve nodded her head. In truth, she'd known how he felt for some time now, and she was torn. She loved him too. But she just couldn't make herself say the words. She wasn't ready to let go of Jeremiah, and admitting her love for another man seemed like the ultimate betrayal to her deceased husband.

"Gabriel…I…"

*****

Gabriel could see the inner struggle written all over her face. Eve had loved Jeremiah fiercely and she was carrying his boppli. Of course she would have trouble admitting she had feelings for another mann, even though Gabriel was almost certain of her feelings towards him.

"Eve, you don't have to say the words. It is enough that I've said them for now."

Eve felt tears spill down her cheeks and Gabriel tenderly wiped them away, "Don't cry."

"I can't help it. You don't understand…"

"Not what you're feeling, but I understand what you can't say yet. And I'm willing to wait. I'm not going anywhere. If you need more time, more time you shall have."

She cried then, wetting his shirt with her tears as he gently held her in his arms. His heart broke for the turmoil she was going through, but he also knew that in order for her to move forward with her life and be happy in the future, she needed to deal with her emotions now.

He held her, murmuring words of comfort and praying that Gott would bring her peace in the midst of her sorrow. She had such grace and beauty to offer the world, she just needed to heal a bit more. And he would be there holding her hand and helping her through it as best he could. He loved her and would wait until she could return his love. Even if it took longer than he really wanted to wait.

One week later…

Eve woke after a sleepless night and muddled through her morning ablutions. She was tired, her feet were slightly swollen, and no matter what she did, she couldn't get Gabriel's words out of her head.

He'd showed up the day before, just in time for dinner, and after adjusting the bedroom window which had gotten stuck open, he'd suggested they take a small walk together. Eve hadn't been out of the house much because of the oppressive heat. It had been unusually warm as Summer moved into Fall, and coupled with the continued unwarranted advice she kept receiving, she'd been sticking close to home whenever possible.

The downside was that she was going a little bit stir crazy. Except for Gabriel's almost daily visits, she spent her days alone or at the quilt shop. Mostly alone. It was nearing the end of the growing season, and that meant extra work for everyone in the Amish community. Canning. Harvesting. Preparing for the winter that would soon be upon them. Everyone had more than enough work to fill their days and even less time than normal to be visiting standoffish widows like her.

When Gabriel had suggested the walk, she'd eagerly agreed, not realizing until that moment how cooped up she'd been feeling. Or how lonely her life was when he wasn't around. They'd walked along the tree-lined road, holding hands and enjoying the cooler air of the evening. Gabriel kept his pace slow so that she could walk without having to hurry, and it was just one of the many things she appreciated about him.

They stopped after half a mile and leaned against the fence, watching the livestock in the field silently for several long moments. Gabriel finally broke their silence, "Eve, have you given any thought to our conversation last week?"

She didn't have to ask for an explanation. She knew he was talking about the conversation where he'd declared his love for her. She'd thought of nothing else all week long, but she still wasn't ready to share her heart with him. She wasn't ready to betray the love she and Jeremiah had experienced. Not yet.

Instead of replying, she simply nodded. She could feel his eyes watching her and then he sighed, "Still not ready to let go of the past? I get it. I can't say that I understand completely, but I can see that you're still hurting."

He wrapped an arm around her shoulders and hugged her to his side as he led her back towards the haus. She'd thought the subject was closed, but then he'd pulled her around to face him and tipped her face up with a finger beneath her chin.

He searched her face and she watched with wide open eyes as he lowered his mouth to her own and kissed her gently. She held still, warring with herself over whether to respond or react. On one hand, she loved Gabriel and kissing him was amazing. Different from kissing Jeremiah, but none the less exciting.

On the other hand, she couldn't stop thinking she was

betraying Jeremiah's love. Gabriel had sensed her struggle and kept the kiss brief. He'd been very patient with her so far, but his patience came with a price. He continued to remind her that he loved her and would wait until she was ready. "Even if that is months or years down the line. I will wait for you."

Eve sighed and leaned against the doorjamb, her heart heavy and her mind confused. Gabriel was a gut mann and deserved to have someone love him with their entire being. And she wasn't sure if she could ever do that or be what he deserved her to be.

Gott, why is this happening to me? I haven't even finished grieving for Jeremiah, and now you bring another mann into my life? He wants my heart and I know he would gladly accept only part of it, but I would always feel guilty for not giving him my all.

What am I supposed to do? Please show me which direction I'm supposed to go. Please?

Her emotions were a rollercoaster, partially due to her advanced pregnancy, but also because her heart was involved and she couldn't seem to figure out how to love two menner. One who was in heaven, and the other who was physically by her side.

She knew Gabriel was trying not to push, but each time they spent any time together, she could tell he was holding back what he really wanted to say. She knew and yet, she did nothing to encourage him. It's much safer if I just keep my feelings to myself.

She turned away from the view and shut the door, determined to make up for lost time by cleaning the haus from top to bottom. She scrubbed the kitchen floors and then started on the carpets. Her back ached as she beat the rugs with the broom, but she didn't stop. She wasn't due to work at the quilt shop for another three days, and she didn't want to sit around and do nothing, or think about Gabriel.

She cleaned the house, did the laundry, and worked in her garden. By the time the afternoon had gone, she was still battling her emotions where Gabriel was concerned. Working herself so hard hadn't solved anything. I love you.

Gabriel's words continued to echo in her mind. Her only small peace of relief was the knowledge that Gabriel wouldn't be stopping by for until the work week was over. Their construction project was a critical stage and he and the other menner would be staying at the work site for the next several days.

She went to bed that night, just like she would each night in the three weeks to come. Glad that she'd met Gabriel and knowing she loved him in return. But unable to say the words.

End of September…

Eve was just putting the finishing stitches in her most recent quilt when the bell over the front door jingled, and she saw her daed and the bishop step into the shop. Both menner wore very solemn faces and she stood up, dropping the spool of thread from her lap to the floorboards.

"Daed?" she asked hesitantly, looking between their faces for some indication of why they had come to the shop. Together.

"Dochder, I afraid I have received some very disturbing news."

Eve swallowed and placed a comforting hand over her swollen stomach, "News?"

"Jah. The bishop was notified a few minutes ago that there has been an accident involving Gabriel."

Eve reached for the closest quilt stand, her knees wobbling as she found herself thrust back into a nightmare she'd thought was behind her. A mann she loved had been injured. The last time this had happened, he'd died. Gabriel cannot die!

"How badly is he injured?" she asked hoarsely.

The bishop shook his head, "This I do not know. He was transported to the Englisch hospital."

"The hospital?" she asked, her knees giving out as she sank to the floor of the quilt shop.

"Bishop, I told you she was too fragile…"

Eve shook her head and pushed herself back to her feet, "Nee, daed. I'm not too fragile, just shocked. I need to…I mean…" She paused and then looked towards her daed, "I need to go to the hospital."

Her daed didn't argue or try to convince her to rethink her decision. He simply nodded and offered, "I will use the Englischer's phone to call a taxi for you. Come, we'll close up the shop now."

Eve helped him close the blinds and lock the doors. Her heart was in turmoil, worry was her constant companion, and even the feeling of her unborn boppli moving inside of her couldn't make her smile.

The taxi arrived fifteen minutes after being called and she rode to the hospital, wringing her hands and asking Gott to please be merciful where Gabriel was concerned. She couldn't lose him now. She needed to tell him…

"Miss, where shall I drop you off?" the driver inquired as he turned into the hospital grounds.

"Uhm…I don't know."

"I'll take you to emergency then. Just ask the uniformed guard at the desk and they should be able to tell you where your friend is being treated."

Eve nodded and a few minutes later she was stepping out of the taxi and handing the driver the required fare. "Denke."

"Yeah, whatever that means," he told her as he accepted the money.

Eve didn't let his attitude bother her and she entered the hospital, immediately spying the uniformed guard and approaching him hesitantly.

"Can I help you miss?"

Eve nodded, "I'm looking for Gabriel Esh? He was brought here after a construction accident?"

"Are you family?" the guard asked, consulting a clipboard in front of him.

"Nee," Eve shook her head, remembering too late she needed to speak in words he could understand. She cleared her throat and tried again, "I'm not family, but he is my friend…"

The guard's eyes softened and he nodded, "He's in treatment room three. Let me step back and see if it's okay if I bring you back. Your name?"

"Eve King."

"Have a seat. I'll be back in a few minutes."

Eve nodded and found a seat on the orange vinyl chairs that seemed completely out of place in the otherwise sterile white environment. She clasped her hands in her lap and tried not to let her worry show.

The guard came back a few minutes later and waved her towards him, "You can go back now." He led her to a small alcove with a curtain pulled across it. "Go on in and have a seat. Your friend is in x-ray right now, but he'll be back in a few minutes."

Eve pushed aside the curtain and took a seat in the only chair in the room. She let her eyes take in the various pieces of medical equipment and felt her fear ratchet higher. I just need to see that he's okay.

She closed her eyes, rubbing a hand absently over her stomach as much to comfort her unborn boppli as to comfort herself.

Please, Gott. I know I've been angry and hurt…but please don't take Gabriel from me too. I love him so much, and I haven't even told him. I can't lose him too. Please…

A noise at the curtain drew her attention and she opened her eyes to see Gabriel being pushed into the room in a wheelchair. He had a bandage covering most of his forehead, and the pale blue of the hospital gown made him look pale and sick.

"Eve?" he asked, grabbing the nurse's hand and quietly asking her for a few moments alone with his visitor.

"Gabriel!" Eve pushed herself out of the chair and rushed to his side, tears wetting her cheeks as her emotions bubbled to the surface. "I came…"

Gabriel pulled her closer, "Shush, don't cry."

Eve gave a teary laugh, "I can't seem to help it. I was so scared when daed told me you'd been in an accident. I was so afraid I wouldn't get a chance to tell you how I feel."

"How you feel?" he asked, brushing a tear off her cheek with the pad of his thumb.

Eve nodded her head, "I love you so much, but I was afraid to say it out loud because I thought it would make what I felt for Jeremiah seem insignificant. As if I never truly loved him."

"But you don't feel that way now?" Gabriel asked.

Eve shook her head, "Nee, I realize that the heart is capable of many kinds of love. I still love Jeremiah and always will. But I love you as well and I don't want to lose you. I don't want you to have to compromise and wait for me…"

Gabriel smiled, "Does this mean you will marry me?"

Eve was openly crying now and nodded, "Jah. Gabriel Esh, I will marry you." She tumbled into his arms when he pulled, landing with a small thud as she knocked the air out of his lungs. She tried to right herself, but he simply wrapped his arms around her stomach and kissed her.

Eve quit struggling and gave herself over to the kiss, feeling loved and so happy all of a sudden, she started crying again. This time they were tears of joy. When she could speak once again, she asked, "What happened?"

"A crane collapsed. I didn't move fast enough and fell through the floor and hit my head. It kind of hurts."

Eve looked at the bandage and then into his eyes, "What did the doctor say?"

The doctor stepped inside the room just as she finished speaking and answered her question, "The doctor says his CT looks fine and he can go home. I'm going to write you a prescription for some painkillers as I'm sure you're going to have a terrible headache tomorrow, and you need to take it easy for a few days, but other than that you're good to go."

Gabriel accepted the papers the doctor handed him, "Thank you, doctor."

Eve smiled, not surprised that Gabriel was using Englisch terms so that everyone could understand him. He was a very considerate mann and she would have expected nothing less. And she was now her mann. She and Gabriel were going to get married.

There was only one small question she still had. Concerning the boppli. Gabriel was watching her and after the doctor left, he stood up from the wheelchair and pulled her into his arms once again, "You're worrying again."

Eve blushed and nodded her head, looking down as her stomach kept her from being able to fully hug him. If she'd been an unmarried Amish women, she would have never considered this type of physical contact with someone other than her legally wed husband, but she was a widow and these circumstances were anything other than normal. Gabriel was going to be her husband, and she needed to feel his arms around her, even if they only reached part way right now.

"You're worried about the boppli?" he surmised.
"How did you…"

"Eve, I've come to know you well these last few months. I know the kinner carries Jeremiah's blood, and I would never try to take that away, but I would be honored if you allowed me to raise this little one as my own. To give this boppli my name."

Eve nodded her head, so happy she could barely contain herself. She reached for him as joy filled every part of her being. When the boppli kicked her under the ribs, she gasped and pressed the heel of her hand against the tiny foot, calming the kicking and mentally promising the boppli that all was going to be well now.

She loved Gabriel and he loved her. He was going to marry her, be her helpmate and best friend, and a daed to the kinner she carried. Just like Job, it seemed that Gott was restoring to her all that she'd lost when Jeremiah died.

Middle of May, an hour after dark…

Eve glanced towards the front door once again, listening carefully to the storm that raged outside. When she didn't hear anything but the howling wind and rain hitting the window panes, she bent her head back to the quilt she was piecing together.

She tried not to let herself worry that Jeremiah hadn't come home yet. He'd picked her up from work, as usual, and then told her he needed to visit a shop on the edge of town and check some cabinet measurements. He'd promised to be home in a few hours, and she'd laughingly promised to have his dinner ready and waiting for him.

She'd decided to wait to eat with him, and currently the casserole she'd made was sitting on top of the stove keeping warm. The rain had started up a little while after Jeremiah had left, and when a loud crack of thunder shook the haus, she put her quilt pieces down and walked to the large window.

She could see the drive and the storm as it moved around her. This was the first summer storm they'd had, and almost three weeks earlier than normal. She briefly wondered how her corn was holding up, it was barely a foot off the ground, and even a strong wind was liable to bend the stocks over. But as much as she wondered, she wasn't inclined to step out in the storm to check it out.

As one hour passed into the next, Eve began to grow worried.

Jeremiah was always punctual and it was so unlike him to be gone for this long, she grew anxious. The storm had abated somewhat, but still Jeremiah did not come home.

When she could stand the worrying no longer, she pulled a quilt around her shoulders, grabbed the lantern sitting by the front door, and headed towards the her parents' haus. It was mile walk through the fields, and she was muddy and soaked through by the time she stood shivering on their front doorstep.

She knocked on the door loudly, hating the fact that she was waking them from their slumber, but knowing there was something wrong. Her daed answered the door, took one look at her, and hollered for her mamm to join him.

After telling him about Jeremiah's errand and failure to come home, her daed hitched the horse up to the buggy and headed towards the emergency phone some two miles away. Her mamm took her into the kitchen and heated water for tea, offering her a towel to dry herself with.

Eve spent forty-five minutes trying to concentrate on the mundane topics her mamm used to try and keep her from worrying, and by the time her daed returned, she was a nervous wreck. He entered the house, a look on his face she'd never seen before.

"Dochder…," he paused at a loss for words. Her mamm seemed to understand what he wasn't saying and she started crying. Eve looked at her and then back to her daed, "What's wrong?"

"Eve, there was an accident. The state police are on their way here…," the sound of car doors slamming stopped his speech. "That will be the police now." He turned and Eve had a horrible feeling in the pit of her stomach. "Daed?" she called after him, dread filling her heart as her mamm continued to cry softly.

"Eve, these are the men from the State police. They need to speak with you about Jeremiah." Her daed made that statement very stiffly, holding back his emotions.

Eve looked to the men, moving her gaze back and forth between theirs. They looked very sorrowful and she whispered, "You know where Jeremiah is?"

One of the officers stepped forward, "Mrs. King, it is with great sorrow that I must inform you…your husband was involved in an buggy accident this evening."

Eve felt her heart stop and she clasped her hands at her throat, "Where is he? Is he hurt?"

"Mrs. King, one of the wheels on the buggy misaligned and caused the buggy to overturn."

Eve nodded as such accidents were known to happen from time to time. Usually the occupants of the buggy suffered only minor scrapes and bruises, occasionally a broken bone. "Thank you for coming to tell me. Was he in need of medical attention?" That was the only reason she could come up with for why Jeremiah had not allowed them to bring him home.

"Mrs. King, your husband's injuries from the buggy accident were only minor, but his buggy overturned at the junction between the highway and the road leading into town. With the storm and the rain…a large delivery truck wasn't able to brake in time to avoid hitting him."

Eve gasped and she saw her daed and mamm reach for her as she crumpled to the floor. "Where…Jeremiah…," she sobbed, unable to speak for the sorrow that was breaking her heart in two.,

"Ma'am, I'm sorry, but her didn't make it. Your husband is dead."

Your husband is dead. The words replayed in her head as the sound of her anguished cry filled the small kitchen. She vaguely heard her daed thank the officers and make arrangements for the body to be brought back to the local undertaker.

Her mamm tried to console her, but Eve felt like a part of her had died. They had both been so happy. Gott, why?

Her mamm helped her upstairs to her old room, helping her remove her apron and muddy shoes. Her mamm helped her change into a borrowed nightgown, poured some water onto a cloth and wiped her face for her, but the tears just kept coming.

Eve knew she needed to get control of herself, but she couldn't come up with a reason to do so. Her mamm sat by her bedside throughout the night, and Eve cried herself to sleep over and over again.

When the first beams of the sun peeked through the window, her eyes were puffy from crying, her body ached, and her stomach was protesting even the slightest movements. Her head ached from crying so hard and for so long.

"Eve, you need to get up and wash your face. I'll bring you some clothes to put on. Come downstairs to breakfast and we'll see what needs to be done." Her mamm's words were soft, and she could feel the love behind them, but Eve simply wanted to stay in bed and let the world go on without her. How am I supposed to do anything without Jeremiah by my side?

She put on the clothing her mamm brought her, but she made no other effort to make herself look presentable. She refused to eat anything, and when the elder council arrived to go over the details of Jeremiah's funeral, she simply got up from the table and walked out the back door.

She walked home without really remembering doing so. Her daed had called her back, even sending her bruder after her, but she ignored them both. She arrived home half an hour later, told her bruder to go home, and locked herself inside.

She headed for the bedroom, but the thought of lying in the bed she'd shared with Jeremiah was much too painful. She pulled the quilt from the bed, hugging it to her and savoring the lingering smell of her husband.

She curled up on the couch, crying herself into a fitful sleep on and off throughout the day. Sometime in the afternoon, she woke up and drank a glass of water and ate a piece of the bread she'd made the day before.

Several people came to her front door, but she ignored them all. When the sun set and the rooms grew dark, she lit a single lantern and lay on the couch and cried herself to sleep once again. The second and third days after her world fell apart, were much the same as the first.

Her familye tried to get her to open the door and to come with them to the funeral service for Jeremiah, but Eve couldn't do it. There was no way she could sit through a lengthy sermon and then watch her husband's body be lowered into the ground. Just the thought of having to witness such a thing caused her another bout of tears and crying.

Her parents were disappointed in her, she could tell by the tone of their voices through the door, but her grief was so great she didn't care. People came and left food gifts on the front doorstep, and she waited until they had left before opening the door and bringing them inside. She just couldn't stand the thought of seeing anyone right now.

End of November…

Gabriel paced the hallway of the hospital, this time his presence there was for a different reason. The birth of his first kinner.

Eve had gone into labor while he was downstairs getting a follow-up head scan, her water breaking and her contractions coming very closely together for a first birth. The doctors at the hospital had insisted on monitoring her for a bit before allowing her to leave, and it was a good thing they had done so.

Thirty minutes later, the boppli's heartrate had dropped dangerously low and the decision had been made to perform a C-section to eliminate the risk to both Eve and her kinner. Eve had been in so much pain, she'd simply nodded and Gabriel had signed the paperwork.

They had been married at the end of October, deciding to wait until most of the harvest was in before drawing their friends and family away from their chores for the day. Since Gabriel had no home of his own, Eve and he had decided to live in the haus that Jeremiah had built. Eve knew that if Jeremiah were able to speak to them from heaven, he would be happy about their decision. She was.

The door opened and Gabriel turned to see a smiling delivery nurse standing there. ""Congratulations, daddy. It's a girl!"

Gabriel nodded and stepped into the room as they wheeled Eve in, their daughter cradled in a nurse's arms. The nurse deposited the small boppli in his arms, whispering,

"Momma going to be in and out for the next few hours. She can hold the baby, but only if someone is right there to help."

"I understand," he said, never taking his eyes off the small person. He moved the blanket and counted the fingers and toes, looking up to see Eve awake and watching him with a small smile upon her face.

"Isn't she beautiful?" she asked him, moving her eyes to her sleeping dochder.

"Jah. Just like her mamm." Gabriel deposited the kinner in Eve's arms and then silently offered up his thanks to Gott above. He not only had a beautiful, amazing fraa to call his own, but he had a healthy dochder as well. "What shall we name her?" he asked, brushing a fingertip down the soft cheek.

Eve did the same and then whispered, "How about Susan?"

Gabriel nodded, "That is a gut name. Susan it is."

He sat on the edge of the bed, his small familye all together. It was such a gut feeling, knowing that everyone was healthy, he found himself smiling and he couldn't stop. He kissed the top of Eve's head and met her eyes, seeing the love he had for her echoed back at him. All was well in the world. All was well with his familye.

I would like to thank you for taking the time to read my book. I really hope that you enjoyed it as much as I enjoyed writing it.

I have been writing Amish books for Amazon for almost two years now, almost exclusively on Kindle. However, due to growing demand I managed to get the majority of my titles available in paperback versions. There is a list of all of my kindle books below, bit by bit they are ALL going to be released in paperback so please keep checking them.

If you feel able I would love for you to give the book a short review on Amazon.

If you want to keep up to date with all of my latest releases then please like my Facebook Page, simply search for Hannah Schrock author.

Many thanks once again, all my love.

Hannah.

LATEST BOOKS

DON'T MISS HANNAH'S BRAND NEW *MAMMOTH AMISH MEGA BOOK* - 20 Stories in one box set.

Mammoth Amish Romance Mega Book 20 books in one set

Outstanding value for 20 books

OTHER BOX SETS

Amish Romance Mega book **(contains many of Hannah's older titles)**
Amish Love and Romance Collection

MOST RECENT SINGLE TITLES

The Orphan's Amish Teacher
The Mysterious Amish Suicide
The Pregnant Amish Quilt Maker
The Amish Caregiver
The Amish Detective: The King Family Arsonist
The Amish Gift
Becoming Amish
The Amish Foundling Girl
The Heartbroken Amish Girl
The Missing Amish Girl
Amish Joy
The Amish Detective
Amish Double
The Burnt Amish Girl

AMISH ROMANCE SERIES

AMISH HEARTACHE

AMISH REFLECTIONS: AMISH ANTHOLOGY COLLECTION

MORE AMISH REFLECTIONS : ANOTHER AMISH ANTHOLOGY COLLECTION

THE AMISH WIDOW AND THE PREACHER'S SON

AN AMISH CHRISTMAS WITH THE BONTRAGER SISTERS

A BIG BEAUTIFUL AMISH COURTSHIP

AMISH YOUNG SPRING LOVE BOX SET

AMISH PARABLES SERIES BOX SET

AMISH HEART SHORT STORY COLLECTION

AMISH HOLDUP

AN AMISH TRILOGY BOX SET

AMISH ANGUISH

SHORT AMISH ROMANCE STORIES

AMISH BONTRAGER SISTERS 2 - THE COMPLETE SECOND SEASON

AMISH BONTRAGER SISTERS - THE COMPLETE FIRST SEASON

THE AMISH BROTHER'S BATTLE

AMISH OUTSIDER

AMISH FORGIVENESS AND FRIENDSHIP

THE AMISH OUTSIDER'S LIE

AMISH VANITY

AMISH NORTH

AMISH YOUNG SPRING LOVE SHORT STORIES SERIES

THE AMISH BISHOP'S DAUGHTER

AN AMISH ARRANGEMENT

AMISH REJECTION

AMISH BETRAYAL

THE AMISH BONTRAGER SISTERS SHORT STORIES SERIES

AMISH RETURN

AMISH BONTRAGER SISTERS COMPLETE COLLECTION

AMISH APOLOGY

AMISH UNITY

AMISH DOUBT

AMISH FAMILY

THE ENGLISCHER'S GIFT

AMISH SECRET

AMISH PAIN

THE AMISH PARABLES SERIES

THE AMISH BUILDER

THE AMISH PRODIGAL SON

AMISH PERSISTENCE

THE AMISH GOOD SAMARITAN

Also Out Now:

The Amish Caregiver

If there's one thing Eve has always been good at, it's caring for those around her. Whether it's her family, neighbors in the Amish community in which she lives, or even the animals on her farm. Eve is first to offer help thanks to her kind and giving heart.

When a terrible storm causes a young Englischer named Oliver to crash his car on the road outside her house, it's Eve's instinct to act as caregiver. As she nurses him back to health, she finds herself growing attached to him - but her heart is torn apart when he has to leave.

Will Eve ever be able to put her feelings for Oliver aside once he goes back to his life in the Englisch world? Or does Gott have a grander plan for the two of them?

Here is a Taster:

"Mamm, you must try to drink some more broth."

Eve sighed as her mother turned her head from the spoon offered her. She was eating less and less every day. Eve prayed, as she had so many times a day, that Gott would spare her. The prayer was a constant one. Almost like breathing. In and out. Spare my mother. In and out. Spare my mother.

For years, Eve had been caring for everyone and everything around her. Her parents would smile lovingly whenever she brought home a bird with a broken wing, or insisted a stray cat stay with them. Sometimes it would become too much even for them, loving people though they were. "This house has become a zoo," her Mamm would say with a furrowed brow. But as soon as she saw the look of pure hope on her daughter's face, Ruth Lantz would smile. She had known how rare it was for a person to be so totally dedicated to the welfare of others.

"Gott has a special plan for all of our lives," Ruth would say, pulling Eve toward her for an affectionate hug. "I believe He wishes for you to help others when they are most in need."

Eve had taken that to heart. Whenever a member of their community became ill, she was the first at the door to offer her services. Even if it was something as simple as helping with chores so the family didn't fall behind, or preparing food to take to the sick person. She had helped nurse little Noah Yoder back to health when he had a grievous cough and fever.

Perhaps if she had been born into the world of the Englisch, she would have studied to be a doctor. She thought about that sometimes, what it would be like to learn all the mysteries of the body and how to heal a person's every illness. How exciting that might be. But only Gott should know such things. He knew best. It was merely up to people to do His work. Too much knowledge, and a person might begin to think they knew better than Gott.

Still, as she sat at her dying mother's bedside, Eve wished there were more she could do.

Mamm was holding up well, though. She was bearing her illness with the same strength and faith which had carried her throughout life. She was never without a kind word on her lips or a prayer in her heart. Oftentimes, she and Eve would pray together.

Eve wiped her mother's brow. She had fallen asleep, her chest rising and falling in shallow breaths. It was only a matter of time.

She took the opportunity to fetch a fresh basin of water and clean towels. Downstairs, her Daed was sitting by the hearth. It was unusual for him to be indoors in the early afternoon—normally, he would have been outside with his son, Caleb, and the farm hands.

"Daed?" Eve placed a gentle hand on her father's shoulder. He seemed to have aged years in only the few short weeks since receiving the news of his wife's cancer. "Can I do anything for you?"

He did not look up at her, but gently patted her hand. "No, thank you, dochder. You are doing so much already. It is a comfort to me that you care so well for your mother in these final days." So he had accepted the fact of his wife's impeding death. For days, he hadn't. He had prayed more fervently than all the rest, sure that Gott would hear him and cure his beloved wife.

"Perhaps you should go and speak with her," Eve said. "She is sleeping at the moment, but she never sleeps for very long. The pain is too great. Every time she moves it wakes her."

He let out a shuddering sigh, and Eve wondered if she had misspoken. For some reason, though she had always thought of her father as the strongest man in the world, it appeared as though she was even stronger than him. It was a strange feeling.

"I will see her shortly. I must go out and help Caleb with the plowing." He sighed. He patted Eve's shoulder. "You are a blessing to us."

Eve didn't see it that way at all. She was merely doing what she felt compelled to do. Her parents had worked hard for years to ensure that Eve and her younger brother lived a good life and had their needs met. The least Eve could do was to care for her mother.

Neighbors visited throughout the day, checking on Ruth and asked how Eve was getting along in her caregiving. "You must take time to rest," Mrs. Lapp said, holding a hand to Eve's forehead as though to check for temperature. Eve only smiled and assured her family's closest neighbor that she was doing well and getting all the rest she needed. Inside, she reminded herself that she didn't need as much rest as an older person might. She was young, only eighteen, and strong. She had the fortitude to spend the long, sleepless nights by her mother's bedside in case she needed anything. Ruth had been moved to Eve's bedroom, so she might be more comfortable and not disturb her husband, who needed to be up before the sun to attend to the needs of the farm.

After a while, it was just Eve and Ruth again. The others were kind to visit, but they had their own families and homes to attend to. The evening meal would have to be prepared.

"Eve." It was a thin whisper, one which Eve had to lean close to hear.

"Yes, Mamm?"

"I am glad you are my dochder. You have a gift for caring. Use that to help others, but take care of yourself, too. Do not wear yourself down. And always put Gott first."

Eve nodded, tears filling her eyes. Her mother's breathing had become more labored. Just the act of speaking so few words had exhausted her.

She took the chance, running downstairs and out the door to call for her father and brother. The time had come—somewhere inside, she knew it.

By the time they reached Ruth's bedside, it was too late.

Two Years Later

Eve jumped at the sound of thunder. She peered out the window over the sink, where she washed the supper dishes. Rain fell so hard and fast; it was impossible to see anything but sheets of water.

The storm was bound to be a terrible one. All day, dark, angry clouds had raced across the sky. The air had fairly crackled with electricity, somehow feeling heavier. Anyone accustomed to summer storms knew there was a strong one brewing.

The thunder boomed again, this time accompanied by a zigzagging bolt of lightning. Eve's heart raced, though she knew she was far too old to be afraid of a silly storm. She would have felt better had her father and brother been inside the house with her, but the odds were they were in the barn, tending to the horses. The animals became so easily spooked at times like that.

She dried her hands on a towel, then took the chance to stepping outside to the covered porch. Rain pounded on the roof over her head, sounding like thousands of thudding hooves. A stampede. It was almost enough to make her cover her ears. She narrowed her blue eyes, hoping to catch a glimpse of her father or Caleb in the downpour. She could see nothing in the heavy rain.

She looked down at the ground beyond the porch. Water was already rising. This is terrible, she thought. Her garden might be drowned, to say nothing of the crops. She hoped it was a strong but fast-moving storm.

A sound floated to her ears just above the cacophony of thudding rain. Even looked back out toward the barn. There was someone there, waving his arms. Daed. He needed her help.

Thinking nothing of herself, Eve took off at a run. Instantly, she was soaked to the skin thanks to the downpour. She shielded her eyes from the driving rain, praying nobody was hurt.

"What is it?" she yelled, hoping to be heard over the storm.

"The horses! We weren't finished bringing them in before it started!" Sure enough, four of them were running loose in the paddock, terrified by the crashing thunder. "We have to get them into the barn!"

Eve nodded, turning to the paddock fence. It was dangerous to approach a spooked horse, but she had built quite a rapport with their horses over the years. She had a gentle nature which they responded to. Reminding herself to be calm, she shimmied through a small opening in the gate.

"Come, Lady," she said, holding one hand to her favorite mare. "Come."

The horse sniffed her hand, and she patted its head. Taking the reins, she led her to the barn, where Caleb was waiting.

They took turns, she and Caleb, calming then leading the horses inside. Rain ran down her face and beat down her back. Her shoes sank into the mud, making it more difficult to even lift her feet from the ground. It was hard work to say the least. Eve wiped water from her eyes, looking forward to getting back inside where it was dry and comfortable. The hem of her dress was covered in mud. It would have to be soaked, along with her muddy stockings.

A bolt of lightning cut across the sky, making the horse Eve was leading rear up on its hind legs. For a brief moment, she was terrified by the thrashing hooves. Then she remembered to keep calm, that nothing would happen to her as long as she remained calm and loving toward the animal.

Daed made a move toward them, as though to help her, but Eve held him off. It would only upset the horse more if he felt as though he were being surrounded.

"Peace, Clover! Peace! There, there." She ran a gentle hand over the horse's muzzle, scratching him behind the ears. Then she continued to lead him the extra hundred yards to the barn while her father closed the paddock gate.

"Eve, the nerve you have!" Daed laughed. "You might have missed your calling. A horse trainer might have been what you were meant to be!"

Eve blushed. She didn't think much of her accomplishment. She just seemed to know what the horse needed.

"Get back to the house," he said, frowning. "I do not want you to become ill, out in the storm this way. I disliked even having to ask you to help."

"That is what I am here for, Daed," she said, smiling. "We work as a family, right?" She turned away and dared the walk back to the house. She didn't run—it was pointless, as she was already soaked through. It was difficult enough to keep her footing, besides, in the slippery mud.

The rain had let up a bit, allowing Eve a better look around the land. Her family's home wasn't set far back from the road. And out there, just beyond the fence separating their land from the neighbors, was a pair of blinking lights.

Eve stopped, waiting to see if they would move. It seemed as though a car was stuck, perhaps in mud off the side of the road. Now the rain didn't matter—it fell on her head, trickled down her face, but it was no matter. She wanted to see whether the driver would leave the car, stopped as it was by the big tree.

Daed and Caleb were still in the barn. Eve went alone to see whether the driver was in need of assistance—her father and brother were strong. Maybe they could push the car out of the mud. She ran to the road, slipping with every step.

When she reached the road, she saw a set of dark marks leading to where the car had settled. As though the driver lost control and the car spun. Eve ran to the car, now fearful. A man was slumped against the wheel, blood trickling down his head.

She looked up, screaming Caleb's name. When he appeared outside the barn, she screamed again. "He needs help!" She tried the door, pulling the handle, but it wouldn't budge.

Moments later, Daed and Caleb came on the run. They assessed the situation, trying all of the doors on the car. It took the two of them working in unison to pull the door beside the driver open.

Eve trotted behind them as they carried the man to the house. He was unconscious, his head still bleeding. They took him to the spare bedroom, laying him carefully down.

"See if he has other injuries," Eve fretted behind them.

"Wait outside," her father ordered. "We will check him over. I do not wish for you to see anything improper." Eve stood outside the room, frustrated. She had no desire to do anything except help the injured man. She listened while the two men checked his arms, legs, beneath his shirt for bleeding or bruising.

"He seems all right, come in." Eve returned. "There is a cut on his forehead, and a few additional scratches. No broken bones, it seems." Caleb stood back, pondering. He might have wounds inside, though, might he not?"

Daed nodded, grim. "Go down to the telephone shanty, Caleb. Call the hospital, ask for an ambulance. He should be looked at by a doctor."

Caleb left in a hurry. Eve saw him running for the road through the bedroom window. The rain was still coming down in buckets, the sky growing darker as night approached.

"I'll get towels, Daed. Some clothing from Caleb's room, maybe? He is shivering."

"Yes, do. I will change him. Caleb can help me when he returns." Eve dashed around the house, getting things together. She also poured hot water into a basin, to wash the man's forehead. There was blood all down the side of his face, too.

By the time she returned to the bedroom, Caleb was running up the stairs. He was winded, and bent at the waist to catch his breath.

"No…phone…lines are down." He panted for air.

"The phone isn't working?" Daed asked. Caleb shook his head.

"The lines have been brought down by the storm. I cannot reach the hospital. I don't believe an ambulance could make it here, even if I got through. Trees are blocking the road as far as the eye can see, in both directions."

The three of them stared at each other, then one by one they turned to the man in the bed.

Daed spoke up. "I suppose he will need to stay with us until we can make it through."

Eve left the bedroom once again while Daed and Caleb dressed the man in dry clothing. He was nearly Caleb's size, so his clothing would fit near enough. While they worked, Eve changed out of her own wet clothing, setting her muddy dress to soak before returning with an oil lamp to the spare bedroom.

He was still unconscious. Eve sat by his side, placing a wash cloth in the water basin before applying the cloth to the stranger's face. There was a lot of dried blood, and Caleb had to empty the basin and refill it before everything was washed away. Then she sat, quiet. She wondered about him. Where had he come from? Where was he going when his car crashed?

"I suppose we should take shifts," Paul Lantz suggested. Eve looked up at her Daed, eyes wide.

"I will take the first shift," she said, almost out of instinct. It was part of her, the need to care for others. It was that need which had brought her to the stranger's car—the need to know whether there was any way to help the man.

He shook his head, his long beard shaking back and forth with him. "I don't think that would be a wise idea, leaving you alone with a stranger—an Englischer, at that."

Eve smiled. "I don't think any harm will come to me. The man is unconscious. He can't move, let alone assault me in any way."

He laughed at her saucy tone. "Fair enough."

"I will take the second shift," Caleb offered. Eve promised to wake him in three hours, though she thought she might allow him to sleep a little longer. He needed the rest more than she did—everybody worked hard on a farm, but the labor of the men was more physically demanding. At least, Eve thought so. She did better with less sleep than her father or brother.

Once she was alone with him, Eve had the chance to think. Everything had happened so fast. Only an hour or so earlier, she was washing dishes and watching the storm. The storm still raged, but now she sat at the bedside of a sick man.

A sick man who happened to be very handsome.

Her cheeks flushed at the turn her thoughts had taken, but there was no denying them. With his face cleaned of blood, except for the little bit seeping through the bandage Eve applied once he was cleaned up, it was clear that he was a very nice looking man. He might have been the most handsome man she'd ever seen. There were a few nice looking young men in her community, one or two of whom she had stolen glances at during church meetings or gatherings. None of them held a candle to the stranger.

His eyes were closed, naturally, and his long, thick eyelashes fell on his cheeks. They seemed to go on forever. His jaw was firm, square. His nose was fine and straight. His hair was thick and dark, swept back from his forehead.

She looked at his eyes again, wishing they were open. Not only would that mean he was awake, naturally, but Eve would be able to see so much more of the person he was inside. It was so easy to tell what a person was like by looking into their eyes.

She wondered what color his eyes were, too.

Then, she shook herself. It was silly, having thoughts like these. Not only that, but they were bound to lead in a direction she knew she should not stray toward. She was thinking about him in a way she shouldn't think about any man, except the man she was to marry.

It was doubly wrong to think this way about an Englischer. He was from another world, far removed from the ways of the Amish like herself. His world was forbidden to her, full of temptation which would only serve to lead her away from Gott.

Still, it was nearly impossible not to be interested in him, to wish she could speak to him. All she had to do was sit by his bedside. Her mind wandered on its own.

Did he have girlfriends? She was sure he must, somebody as handsome as he was. There had to be plenty of girls all over him. She knew how free and easy girls behaved in the Englisch world. She couldn't even wear her blonde hair down in public, or leave it uncovered. Yes, the girls were probably crazy about him.

She told herself it wasn't wrong to have these thoughts, since the stranger was sick and unconscious. As long as they didn't go any further, she wouldn't have anything to feel guilty about.

He stirred fretfully. She leaned over him, placing a hand on his forehead to soothe him. She wanted to be sure he wasn't running a fever, too. She knew that some illnesses could lead to fever and infection if left unchecked. He was cool to the touch, and Eve thanked Gott for it. If he were badly injured inside, there would be nothing she could do for him.

He had a strong, fine body. It was unlikely that he worked on a farm, the way her brother did, though their builds were very much the same. He might have been an athlete. In any case, he was a very active person who took care of himself.

Not for the first time did she ask herself where he was supposed to be. She wondered if the people there were worried over him. She would have been, in their shoes, knowing he was on his way during a fierce storm. The rain still fell, and the wind had picked up. It made the windows rattle in their casements. She shuddered to think of the condition of the farm by the time the rain stopped. There would be a lot of work to do.

And there was him. The stranger. She wondered if he would be with them for very long. How long would it take before the roads were cleared? Daed and Caleb could take him to the hospital in the buggy if need be, if the telephone lines weren't up in time to call for an ambulance.

The Amish Caregiver

Also Out Now:

The Amish Detective: The King Family Arsonist

Gloria Kauffman's world has been turned upside down. Her beloved cousin, Susan King, died three days ago in a house fire which also claimed her parents and twin brothers. The entire family is in mourning, and the community is shaken to the core when the police determine the fire was an act of arson. Who would commit such a heinous crime? And who will be next?

At the service, Gloria meets Detective Paul Miller, a young man whose determination to solve the case is second only to hers. They join together to investigate the crime and develop a bond that dangers on forbidden love.

Gloria believes there's something suspicious about the crime. The King family were nothing but good, generous, pious Amish people. Who would have wanted to hurt them, and why?

It isn't long until Gloria finds out the sad, shocking and terrible truth - and that truth might come at the cost of her life.

Here is a Taster:

Gloria sat in the corner of the barn, wiping tears from her eyes as members of the Ordung filed through, one by one, to pay their respects to a beloved family.

It all seemed like a nightmare, one Gloria wished she could awaken from. The last three days had all been part of that nightmare. Everything changed the moment her family received word of the fire. By then, most of their neighbors already knew the story. Life had been spent in a haze since then.

It wasn't just the fact of the fire that worried members of the Ordung, both the communities in which she and her extended family lived. It was the way the fire took place. The police stated it was a clear case of arson, meaning that someone had deliberately started the fire which killed her aunt, uncle and three cousins in their sleep.

Neighbors were in an uproar, and rightly so. How could they protect themselves from this arsonist? Who would be next? There was no question that the act was random—the Kings had no enemies. That simply wasn't the way of the Amish. And they spent very little time outside the community, so there was only limited involvement with the Englischers in town. It wasn't plausible that some person Isaac King knew or did business with would go so far as to set fire to the home. It had to be a sad, troubled person who felt the need to hurt others.

Who would they hurt next?

It was heartbreaking, seeing the pain on the faces of friends and neighbors as they paid their respects. Isaac, a good and hardworking farmer. He had been so well-loved. Esther, always ready with a helping hand and a gentle smile. The two of them had been a strong couple, their commitment to one another second only to their commitment to Gott. There they were. Like second parents to Gloria for as long as she could remember. Both of them in their simple wooden caskets.

Then there were the other three caskets, and Gloria's heart broke a little further when she picked her cousin Susan's out from the three. Susan who was more like a sister to Gloria than a cousin. Whose loyalty and devotion never wavered. Gloria had always wanted to be more like Susan, who was endlessly patient and good to everyone she knew. She had never so much as told a lie, and now she was gone.

And the smaller caskets. Jacob and Elijah, the twins. Only ten years old. They would never grow up to be good men like their father. It seemed as though tears would never stop flowing from Gloria's eyes.

It was worse for her mother, Uncle Isaac's younger sister. She was inconsolable—throughout the days following the fire, Gloria had woken in the middle of the night to the sound of her mother's tears. It seemed as though they might never end.

It was true that faith in Gott that helped the Amish through difficult times, but this was far beyond anything anyone had ever encountered. Not just grief, which everyone must face at one time or another, but fear of the unknown. An Amish person's life generally fell into a distinct, routine pattern. This terrible tragedy had destroyed that pattern.

Even from her quiet corner seat, Gloria overheard the grumblings of several of the community's most respected leaders. They were considering holding a meeting to form teams of men to keep watch on the homes and farms of their neighbors. Never had anything like this been considered in the past. Gloria felt somehow as though so much of what she loved about her life was slipping away. The peace, tranquility, trust. It was the same for all the others. Would they even have a decent night's sleep while waiting to see whose home was next?

"Gloria, are you well?" One of the neighbors, Mrs. Stolztfus, approached.

"As well as can be, thank you," she replied. Her heart wasn't in her words. She felt cold inside.

"Your Mamm seems to be holding up well, all things considered."

"Yes, all things considered." It wasn't in Gloria's nature to be short or sharp, especially with one of her elders, but the older woman couldn't seem to get the message that she didn't wish to speak. It was all too strenuous. Even basic conversation was too much.

"You and your cousin Susan were very close, I know. I remember when you were just little girls, running barefoot along the outside of your home."

Gloria clenched her fist to keep from crying out loud. Didn't Mrs. Stoltzfus understand she was causing pain? Maybe, one day, it would be possible to sit and think of Susan and smile. Maybe Gloria would be able to reminisce about the times she spent with her sweet cousin and remember them fondly, instead of wishing them back with all her might. If only she could go back.

Mrs. Stoltzfus clicked her tongue in sympathy. "To think of something like this happening to Isaac King, of all people. Only the most pious person anyone had ever known, and the friendliest. If it could happen to him, it could happen to any of us."

Gloria had heard it all before, whispered and murmured from one neighbor to another. She gave the same response she had for days. "We must trust in Gott."

"Of course, of course. I only wish the person responsible were caught for what they did. I'm sure it would be easier for your poor Mamm to get over the loss of her brother if she knew the person who took his life was behind bars, where he could hurt no one else."

Then, she walked away, and Gloria couldn't help but breathe a sigh of relief. She had felt suffocated by the older woman's presence. The air felt clearer, cooler.

Why did people feel the need to cloak their curiosity and own selfish need to fret and worry under the mask of care? Gloria knew her neighbor was only venting her fear, and maybe even relishing the excitement of the situation—morbid though that was. Why couldn't people behave that way amongst themselves and leave those who mourned alone with their grief?

Susan's casket. Gloria's eyes kept falling on it. She remembered the gold of Susan's hair, and the cornflower blue of her eyes. Those eyes that had laughed and sparkled, always full of joy. Gloria would never know another person like her. My life will always be a little darker, she thought.

She thought about what Mrs. Stoltzfus said, too, about Uncle Isaac's piousness and how respected and trusted he had been. It was all true, all of it, and it added just another layer to the shock and horror of the event.

If only I had visited Susan when I said I would. It was something she'd berate herself over for the rest of her life. She was sure of it. If only she hadn't been so busy getting her next quilt ready for sale, she could have spent time with her cousin before…before the fire.

I'll never make a mistake like that again. She would never pass up the opportunity to spend time with her loved ones. Nothing was more important than that. There was no guarantee that any of them would be around tomorrow. If there was nothing else to be taken from the tragedy, Gloria thought, that was lesson enough.

Her father, brothers and sisters all gathered together toward the front of the crowd, near where the caskets sat. She wondered if anyone thought it strange that she sat alone—there was no missing the eyes that had watched her throughout the day. People asking themselves why she sat alone. If they had bothered to ask, she would have told them it was too painful to be near the caskets, even if it meant being near her family. She had to be alone with her thoughts, her grief.

She smoothed a long strand of auburn hair back beneath her kapp. She'd been a little lax with her grooming that day, her mind a million miles away.

Just like Susan was. A million miles away, in Heaven. Of course she was in Heaven. That was the only place a person like her could go.

Gloria wiped another tear, one of many endlessly streaming down her face.

There was a bit of a commotion at the barn doors. Gloria turned to see who had entered, and was surprised to see an Englischer. His tan suit, brown shoes and sunglasses set him apart right away. So did his lack of facial hair, as all men his age in the Amish faith grew beards after baptism.

He looked around the room, removing the glasses in order to see better. In the light from the oil lamps hanging from the rafters, Gloria finally recognized him. He was some sort of a policeman. She had seen him over the last three days, here and there. Normally hanging around on the edges of crowds, looking and listening. It was unnerving, feeling as though she and her people were being observed like that. Unnerving but not unusual, since being watched by Englischers was a fact of life for the Amish. Whenever Gloria went to town to sell her quilts, there was never any shortage of Englischers watching and pointing, whispering behind their hands. They'd even pulled up to her family's home on many occasions in their cars. As though the Amish existed as a form of entertainment.

This man at least seemed respectful. He kept his distance from the group of mourners. He was only going his job, Gloria reminded herself. He wasn't watching out of curiosity. She did wish he would have picked a better time to visit, though.

She couldn't take her eyes from him, even though she knew she should. He was fascinating. And handsome. This was the first chance she'd had to observe him, instead of the other way around. His dark brown hair, the bit of shadow on his cheeks. He looked tired—Gloria thought he must have been spending endless hours on the case, and her heart went out to him. He was trying to find the person responsible for the tragedy which befell her family. It meant more than he knew, she was sure.

He caught the eye of her Daed, who touched his wife's arm to get her attention. She turned and, when she saw the officer, rose from her chair. Gloria stood immediately. It was one thing for a stranger, policeman or no, to be there. It was another for him to bother her mother in her time of grief.

By the time she reached them, he was already asking questions. She heard him say something about additional family members, but her mother shook her head. When she reached them, Gloria placed a concerned hand on her mother's shoulder and turned to face the officer.

His eyes fell on her. "Excuse me, miss, but I have some questions for your mother which I think would be best asked solely of her."

So he knew who she was already. He'd already been asking questions, evidently.

"I'm sure you do, and I would like to hear them for myself." She turned to her mother. "Is that all right?"

"If the detective does not mind."

Gloria turned to the detective and waited with an expectant smile. He must have known there was no way for him to dissuade her, though it was obvious from the way he cleared his throat before speaking that he wasn't over-fond of speaking in front of her.

"Actually, I don't have anything else to ask. I wanted to assure you that we're doing everything in our power to find the culprit behind the crime." He smiled at Gloria. "We've never actually met. I'm Detective Paul Miller."

"Gloria Kauffman," she replied, smiling slightly.

"I'm very sorry for your loss, Miss Kauffman." He smiled at her Mamm and shook her hand. The smile changed his face—he was normally so serious, stern. When he smiled he looked younger. "I'll leave you, now. I'm sorry to have disrupted the wake."

"Would you like to stay for refreshments?" Gloria smiled fondly at her Mamm, who was cordial and kind even in the worst of times.

"No, thank you, ma'am. I'm sure you would rather proceed without the reminder of the police hanging around. Thank you for the offer." He nodded at the two of them and left the barn.

Gloria couldn't stand to see him go without finding out more. She ran after him, not caring who saw. Finding out about the arson was more important.

"Excuse me," she murmured when she caught up to him. She touched him arm purely out of reflex, then pulled her hand back as though he burned to the touch.

He turned back to her. "Yes, Miss Kauffman?"

"Detective, is there any new information about the murderer? Anything at all?"

He frowned. "Miss Kauffman, it's very unusual for a detective to discuss a case with the family of the victim before there's any sure suspect. I can't share speculation with you."

Her frown mirrored his. "But you do know something?"

"I can't tell you either way. I'm sorry, I'm sure it's frustrating. We're just as frustrated at the station, believe me." He turned away as if to go, and she touched his arm again. Again, she felt it was improper, but she was desperate.

"Miss Kauffman, it would be best if you go back in with your family. You need each other at a time like this. Let us do our job, and we'll let you know if there's any further news. You'll be the first to know, in fact." Again, he turned away.

Gloria went around him, standing in his way. He sighed in exasperation.

"I want to help you."

His eyes went wide. They were a deep blue, the color of the sky at twilight. "You what?"

"I want to help. I'm sure there's something I can tell you that you don't already know."

"You mean there are secrets we aren't aware of?"

She blushed and took a step back. "No. I didn't mean it that way."

"How did you mean it, then?"

"I only meant to say that I'm close with the family. Susan was like my sister. We Amish—we're close, anyway. We live our lives together, helping one another. We depend on each other. I'm sure you don't know that."

"I'm sure I don't," he said, with a wry smile.

"So you see, we know a lot about each other. Add to that my closeness with my cousin and, well, you see what I mean. I'm sure I can offer something of value to the investigation."

He looked skeptical, his eyes narrowing. "I'm not sure. We already know a lot about the family. We've spoken to the neighbors, for miles in all directions."

"I grew up with them. I'm sure there's something you've missed. I only want the chance to help."

She felt his eyes on her as he sized her up, and drew herself up to her full height. She was small, especially when compared to his tall height, but she was stronger than she looked. The detective would find that out, if he ever gave her a chance.

"You won't leave me alone until I agree to talk with you, will you?" His face wore a wry smile. He had a dry sense of humor, Gloria noticed.

She had to smile, too. "No, I won't. You'll be saving yourself a lot of time if you just let me have my say. I know you won't regret it."

He shrugged. "All right. What if we meet at the coffee shop tomorrow afternoon?"

The smile faded from her face. "The funeral is tomorrow afternoon."

"Oh. That was clumsy of me."

Gloria swallowed over the lump in her throat. "That's all right. You didn't mean it."

"I plan to be at the funeral as well—standing off to the back, of course. I wouldn't want to get in the way."

This surprised her so much, she forgot the threat of tears. "Why would you do that?"

"It's something we do—the police, I mean. I want to be there to keep an eye out for any suspicious looking people."

"But only the Amish will be there. People like me. You don't think it was someone from the community, do you?"

He winced. "No. And I think that should be as much as we discuss about it. I'll meet up with you after the services are finished."

Gloria's eyes cut toward the barn. She wondered how her family would feel about her running off to meet with an Englischer, detective or not. It was all in the name of getting answers, though.

"All right. I'll look for you."

"I don't think it'll be too tough to find me." He grinned, and Gloria giggled before she could help herself. Yes, he would stand out in his fine suit, so unlike the plain clothes of her people.

She hurried back to the barn, then, fearful of being discovered with the Englischer. Giggling when everyone else was in mourning. The talk would never end.

The Amish Detective: The King Family Arsonist

Made in the USA
Lexington, KY
27 November 2019